BOYS TOWN®
Press

Boys Town, Nebraska

To all the people struggling with sad...
It takes a strong person to ask...

When I couldn't get Over it, I learned to Start Acting Differently

A story about managing SADness

Written by Bryan Smith

Illustrated by Lisa M. Griffin

When I Couldn't Get Over It, I Learned to Start Acting Differently
Text and Illustrations Copyright © 2018 by Father Flanagan's Boys' Home
ISBN: 978-1-944882-22-8

Published by the Boys Town Press
13603 Flanagan Blvd.
Boys Town, NE 68010

For a Boys Town Press catalog, call **1-800-282-6657**
or visit our website: BoysTownPress.org

Publisher's Cataloging-in-Publication Data

Names: Smith, Bryan (Bryan Kyle), 1978- author. | Griffin, Lisa M., 1972- illustrator.

Title: When I couldn't get over it, I learned to start acting differently : a story about managing SADness / written by Bryan Smith ; illustrated by Lisa M. Griffin.

Other titles: Managing SADness.

Description: Boys Town, NE : Boys Town Press, [2018] | Audience: grades K-5. | Summary: Kyle gets the blues all the time. With a little help, he learns how to recognize and manage his sadness by reframing his attitude so he can Start Acting Differently.--Publisher.

Identifiers: ISBN: 978-1-944882-22-8

Subjects: LCSH: Sadness in children--Juvenile fiction. | Depression in children--Juvenile fiction. | Emotions in children--Juvenile fiction. | Attitude change in children--Juvenile fiction. | Self-control in children--Juvenile fiction. | Self-reliance in children--Juvenile fiction. | Children--Life skills guides--Juvenile fiction. | CYAC: Sadness--Fiction. | Depression, Mental--Fiction. | Change (Psychology)--Fiction. | Self-control--Fiction. | Self-reliance-- Fiction. | Conduct of life--Fiction. | BISAC: JUVENILE FICTION / Social Themes / Emotions & Feelings. | JUVENILE FICTION / Social Themes / Self-Esteem & Self-Reliance. | JUVENILE FICTION / Social Themes / Depression & Mental Illness. | JUVENILE NONFICTION / Social Topics / Emotions & Feelings. | JUVENILE NONFICTION / Social Topics / Self-Esteem & Self-Reliance. | EDUCATION / Counseling / General.

Classification: LCC: PZ7.S643366 W54 2018 | DDC: [Fic]--dc23

Printed in the United States
10 9 8 7 6 5 4 3 2 1

Boys Town Press is the publishing division of Boys Town, a national organization serving children and families.

Hey everyone, Kyle here.
I have to be honest and let
you in on a little secret.

Just the other day, I cried
in front of my friends...
well, the kids I thought were
my friends.

Anyway, you heard me right. Me, a fourth-grade boy, cried right in front of the other kids. **I thought my life was ruined.**

It all started at recess about a month ago during what was **supposed** to be a friendly game of touch football.

I'm not very athletic, but I still like to play football. Of course I got picked last, but **I can get over that.** I never get any balls thrown to me, and **I can even get over that, too.**

My team was down by three points. I saw John, our quarterback, and another kid whisper to each other and start laughing.

I wondered what that was about. Then John said,

"Hut," got the ball, and ran right at me.

This was the day I was going to be the hero. All it would take was a soft toss to me and I was going to have my first touchdown!

But that's not what happened.

When John was five feet away from me, he reached back and threw the ball as hard as he could **AT MY FACE!** Next thing I knew, I was laying on the ground with a bloody nose.

I bet you think this is the part when I started crying.

NOPE.

It was just a bloody nose; **I could get over that.**

STAY ACTIVE

RUN · BIKE · DANCE
TEAM SPORT

Here's the weirdest part. Instead of saying they were sorry or checking on me, everyone started laughing. Someone even said,

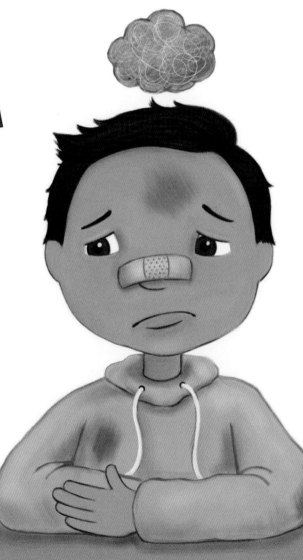

"You shouldn't play football if you don't know how to catch."

I went to the school nurse, but never once shared what really happened. That would only make things worse.

Besides, **I was sure I could get over it.**

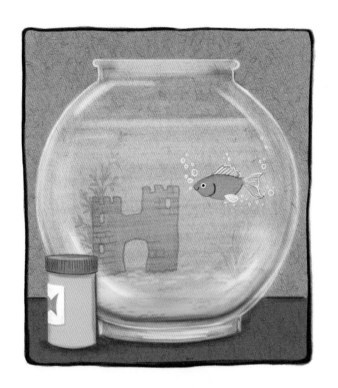

A few days later, Mom and Dad said they had some bad news.

As if being made fun of at school wasn't enough, my parents told me that Bubbles, my pet fish, died. I can't tell you how many times he listened to me when I was having problems.

Checking on Bubbles was one of the best things I looked forward to doing each day.

Why does everything BAD always happen to me?

I have to say, I just wasn't sure how I was **going to get over this.**

Things at school didn't get any better, either. Every day, the boys would point and laugh at me.

14

Next thing I knew, I was playing by myself at recess and eating lunch alone.
I felt like such a loser. One day when the kids were laughing at me, I couldn't
help it. **_I started crying in front of all the fourth-graders._** Now, not only was
I a loser, I was also a crybaby.

How could I possibly get over that?

Here's the thing. I've been sad before, but this was different.
My sadness before would come and go, but not this time.
I began to feel more and more sad, and there was
nothing that could help. I really just felt like

I could not get over it.

I used to love to go outside and play. But now all I wanted to do was go to my room, turn off the lights, and be left alone. I just kept wondering why people are so MEAN, and what I did to deserve their meanness.

After a few weeks, I quit combing my hair and stopped trying in school.

Why does everything bad always happen to me?

NONE of it seemed to matter. Mom and Dad couldn't believe I was still this upset about my fish dying.

If only they knew what else was going on.

Mom and Dad decided to call the school counselor, Mrs. Bell, to see if she could help. Mrs. Bell told me she was already planning to talk to me because two kids in my class had told her I seemed **SAD,** and they weren't sure what to do.

So I met with Mrs. Bell. She told me it was not okay for the kids to laugh and make fun of me, and that she would be addressing that. But she also reminded me that I can't control other people's behavior. I can only control how I deal with it.

Mrs. Bell told me, "When people are this sad, one thing to try is to **Start Acting Differently.** I would like to help you figure out some ways to do just that."

I told Mrs. Bell, **"There really isn't any point. I've turned into such a LOSER and a CRYBABY."**

19

"Whoa," said Mrs. Bell. "That sounds like a lot of negative self-talk."

"Negative self-talk is when a person talks badly about himself or herself," she said. "And you just said you were a loser and a crybaby. What those kids are doing is wrong and **THAT** doesn't make you a loser or a crybaby."

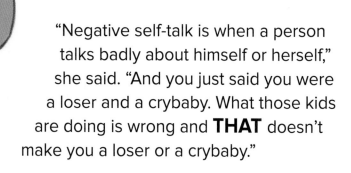

"Now let's talk about some things
you can do to...

**Start
Acting
Differently**

1. When kids are mean to you, tell them how you feel.

2. If they continue, walk away.

3. You can even ask for help from someone you trust if they continue to be mean.

"But most importantly, Kyle, you need to remember that ***there's always hope.***
There are many people who ***care about you*** and want to help you."

"It sure doesn't feel like it."

"I'm sure it doesn't right now but if we work together, I'm sure we can figure it out.
Try these things and let me know if they help."

The next day, when the boys started teasing me at lunch, I decided to tell them how I felt. But they kept on. So I decided it was best to just walk away.

After I took about ten steps, one boy, Dylan, walked up behind me. **Here we go again,** I thought. But instead of teasing me, he said, "Sorry they're being mean to you."

I was shocked.

Did I just hear something nice come out of one of their mouths? **That helped me start to feel a little better.** Isn't it crazy how one person can affect someone's day?

But the rest of the boys continued to tease me every day, so I went back and asked Mrs. Bell for help. Mrs. Bell talked with them — not just about me, but about some other students they were picking on, too. I guess she tried to get them to understand what it felt like.

23

Later, Mrs. Bell asked me why I would want to play with kids who are always so mean to me. I didn't have a good answer; I told her I guess I just wanted to feel popular.

"Having good friends is better than being popular," she said. "Never change yourself to fit in. Just be the best person you can be, and the right people will want to be your friends."

I thought about that for a while.
And I realized that there really wasn't an easy way for me to just get over all of this unless I figured out a way to

Start
Acting
Differently.

I'm feeling better!

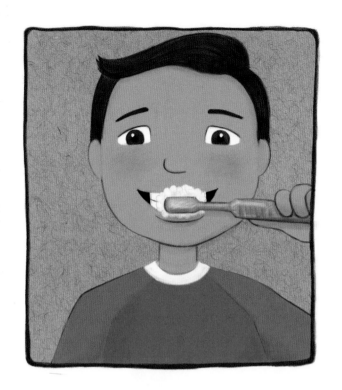

From that day on, I decided to make some changes.

As I looked in the mirror, I didn't like what I saw. I needed a fresh new start. I brushed my teeth (and combed my hair), put on my favorite baseball shirt, and even started working on the math homework I was behind in.

I decided to tell my parents about what was really happening. You know what? They really cared about what was going on. They started helping me see all the good things there are to like about me. I guess I should have talked to my parents at the beginning.

This helped me start feeling even better.

Each day, I started feeling a little happier, too. At school, I decided to not play football at recess because I didn't want to be around people who were mean to me.

28

Instead, I pretended to be an archaeologist who was digging for fossils. A week later, a boy named Mario asked what I was doing. So I told him, and since then, Mario and I have dug for fossils every day and have become great friends.

I know one day I am going to feel sad again, and that I'm not always going to be able to just get over it. But now I know there are things I can do differently. I also know that if nothing else works,

I can ASK FOR HELP.

Mrs. Bell is still working with our class to help make sure this kind of thing doesn't happen to others. But you know what?

If I see kids who seem sad, I'm going to try and help them. If that doesn't work, I'll ask someone I trust to help them.

All it takes is ONE person to Start Acting Differently.

TIPS for Parents and Educators

It's easy for kids to feel sad when bad things happen in their lives. This is especially true when boys and girls are bullied or picked on, or feel left out and isolated. That's why it's so important for children to learn how to deal with difficult times in positive ways so they can be successful at home, in school, and with others.

Here are some tips and suggestions parents and teachers can use to teach kids how to manage sadness and to Start Acting Differently:

1. **Children look to their parents and teachers as role models.** So it's okay to acknowledge your own sadness and help your children/students learn and understand the healthy ways you deal with it.

2. **Remember, perception is reality.** Acknowledge your child's/student's sadness, whether it is big or small.

3. **Sometimes even the smallest actions can make a world of difference.**
- Participate in one of your child's/student's favorite activities. This can help kids get their minds off the sadness for a short time.
- Sometimes kids just want to be heard. Focus on their needs and be an active listener.

4. **Don't wait** for children/students to come to you for help. If a child seems sad, talk to him or her in a private setting about what you are noticing and reassure him or her you are there to help if needed.

5. **Help your child/student learn some coping strategies** to deal with sadness. The **Boys Town National Hotline®** offers a free, printable, customizable list of "99 Coping Skills" at **YourLifeYourVoice.org.**

6. **Be sure to frequently check on children/students** who seem sad to show them someone cares about them.

For more parenting information, visit boystown.org/parenting.

BOYS TOWN® Parenting

YOUR Life YOUR Voice .org is a free Boys Town Hotline website that is available to kids, teens, and young adults. Anyone can call, text, chat, or email to get help if they're sad, depressed, stressed, being bullied, fighting with a friend, a sibling, or a parent, or facing an overwhelming challenge.

 4 WAYS TO GET HELP

TEXT: "VOICE" to 20121   **E-MAIL:** YLYV@boystown.org
CHAT: yourlifeyourvoice.org   **CALL:** 1-800-448-3000

Boys Town Press Featured Titles
Kid-friendly books for teaching social skills

Executive **FUNction**

What Were You **Thinking?**

Written by Bryan Smith
Illustrated by Lisa M. Griffin

978-1-934490-85-3

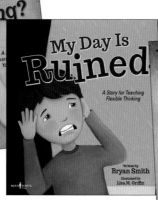

My Day Is Ruined!

A Story for Teaching Flexible Thinking

Written by Bryan Smith
Illustrated by Lisa M. Griffin

978-1-944882-04-4

Of COURSE It's a Big Deal!

A Story about Learning to React Calmly and Appropriately

Written by Bryan Smith
Illustrated by Lisa M. Griffin

978-1-944882-11-2

It Was Just Right Here!

Written by Bryan Smith
Illustrated by Lisa M. Griffin

978-1-944882-20-4

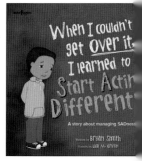

When I couldn't get over it, I learned to Start Acting Different!

A story about managing SADness

Written by Bryan Smith
Illustrated by Lisa M. Griffin

978-1-944882-22-8

Is There an **App for That?**

Written by Bryan Smith
Illustrated by Katie W...

Hailey Discovers HAPPiness through Self-Acceptance

978-1-934490-74-7

Downloadable Activities
Go to BoysTownPress.org to download.

WiTHOUT LiMiTS
dream • connect • soar

Downloadable Activities
Go to BoysTownPress.org to download.

MINDSET MATTERS

Written by Bryan Smith
Illustrated by Lisa Griffin

978-1-944882-12-9

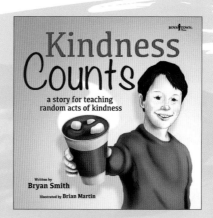

Kindness Counts

a story for teaching random acts of kindness

Written by Bryan Smith
Illustrated by Brian Martin

978-1-944882-01-3

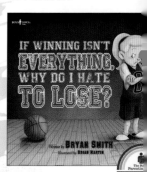

IF WINNING ISN'T EVERYTHING, WHY DO I HATE TO LOSE?

Written by Bryan Smith
Illustrated by Brian Martin

978-1-934490-85-3

BOYS TOWN® Press

For information on Boys Town and its Education Model, Common Sense Parenting®, and training programs:
boystowntraining.org | boystown.org/parenting
training@BoysTown.org | 1-800-545-5771

For parenting and educational books and other resources:
BoysTownPress.org
btpress@BoysTown.org | 1-800-282-665...

.GOODNIGHT.
TRAVERSE CITY

WRITTEN BY MANDY TOOMEY · ILLUSTRATED BY JIM DEWILDT

AMP&RSAND, INC.

Chicago · New Orleans

ISBN 978-0-9985222-7-2

Published by
AMPERSAND, INC.
515 Madison Street
New Orleans, Louisiana 70116

719 Clinton Place
River Forest, Illinois 60305

www.ampersandworks.com

Design: David Robson

Printed in U.S.A.

To request a personalized copy or to schedule a book signing/school reading email
goodnighttraversecity@gmail.com

Ten percent of revenue from sales of this book will be donated to Traverse City Area Public Schools Food Assistance Program which helps pay past due lunch balances for families in need.

The author would like to thank the following:
Dennos Museum Center
   at Northwestern Michigan College
Grand Traverse Pie Company
Mission Point Lighthouse
Moomers Homemade Ice Cream
National Cherry Festival
Prairie School Vineyard
State Theatre and Bijou by the Bay
Traverse City Area Public Schools
Traverse Tall Ship Co.
John and Leslye Wuerfel,
   Traverse City Beach Bums

This book is dedicated to people who love Traverse City, Michigan. Whether you live there full time, rent a cabin for the summer on a lake nearby, visit to see the changing colors of the fall, or ski the white wintery slopes, this book is dedicated to you. It's not just the vast beauty that makes the area so special, but the people who are in it that make Traverse City a one of a kind destination.

Goodnight sparkling water in Grand Traverse Bay

Goodnight M-22, our scenic highway

Goodnight cherry orchards and the blossoms in May

Goodnight Front Street with shops and places to dine

Goodnight Old Mission Peninsula and grapes on the vine

Goodnight Mission Point Lighthouse that's fun to visit

Goodnight Dennos Museum Center and great exhibits

Goodnight Cherry Festival with lots to see and do

Goodnight Cherry Royale Parade and the airshows, too

Goodnight Sleeping Bear Dunes where the climb is so high

Goodnight Grand Traverse Pie Company and delicious cherry pies

Goodnight Tall Ship Manitou

Goodnight Pyramid Point and that spectacular view

Goodnight Open Space where kites fly high all day

Goodnight State Theatre and Bijou by the Bay

Goodnight Moomers and favorite ice cream

Goodnight Beach Bums and cheering for the team

Goodnight sandy beaches and bonfires at night

Goodnight Cherry Capital of the World

Traverse City, sleep tight

TRAVERSE CITY TERMS

Cherries – Over half of all cherries grown in the U.S. come from Michigan. Sweet ones end up in foods like yogurt or ice cream. Tart ones go into pies and other baked desserts. They also can be dried.

Cherry Capital of the World – Peter Dougherty began planting cherry trees in 1852. Soon others followed and cherries became the region's most important crop. Today about 3.8 million tart and 0.5 million sweet cherry trees surround the Traverse City area.

Cherry Royale Parade – Celebrating the area's heritage with the Cherry Queen, floats, marching bands and more.

Dennos Museum Center at Northwestern Michigan College, Traverse City, is the region's premier facility for programming in the visual arts, sciences and performing arts.

Front Street – named one of the *10 Great Streets in America* by the American Planning Association. It won because of the way it functions as a "complete street" which means that pedestrians, cyclists, transit riders and motorists use it equally. City planning, historic preservation and downtown redevelopment were the key reasons for the award.

Grand Traverse Bay is formed by two peninsulas in Lake Michigan. It is 32 miles long, 10 miles wide and up to 620 feet deep in some areas.

Grand Traverse Pie Company is a well respected Michigan brand that has several shop locations serving pie and food. They believe the Power of Pie helps provide healthy futures for children and families by developing compassionate, resilient and mindful communities.

Mission Point Lighthouse operated from 1870 to 1933. Now visitors can see what life was like for lighthouse keepers and others who lived at the end of Old Mission Peninsula.

Moomers Homemade Ice Cream – The "Moomers Experience" exemplifies family. With a family owned and operated business overlooking their 80 acre dairy farm, Moomers shares their passion for ice cream and agriculture alike.

M-22 – This scenic 116.7 mile highway follows the Lake Michigan shoreline and Leelanau Peninsula. It's where you'll find quaint communities, spectacular natural beauty and many points of interest.

National Cherry Festival – An annual festival held in Traverse City since 1926.

Old Mission Peninsula extends into the center of Grand Traverse Bay with 22 miles of beautiful views, vineyards, orchards, forests and villages.

Open Space *Public Square/Plaza* sits right on Grand Traverse Bay and is a major part of the Traverse City park system.

Pyramid Point rises 300 feet from Lake Michigan and is another massive dune of Sleeping Bear legend. The 2.7 mile hiking trail has a high lookout point over Lake Michigan.

Sleeping Bear Dunes – Towering 450 feet above Lake Michigan, the natural world of these dunes includes miles of sand beaches, forests, inland lakes, unique flora and fauna, a lighthouse and beautiful farmsteads. On a clear day you can see across the lake from one of the high dunes.

State Theatre and **Bijou by the Bay** – Located in downtown Traverse City, the State Theatre and Bijou by the Bay are two historic, volunteer-run, community movie theaters operated by the Traverse City Film Festival.

Tall Ship Manitou – At 114 feet, the Tall Ship Manitou is a replica of an 1800s "coasting" cargo schooner. Similar to those that sailed the Great Lakes and Atlantic Ocean, it offers a variety of two-hour cruises for up to 59 passengers during the season.

Traverse City Beach Bums – professional baseball team whose slogan is "To invite the public in as guests, and have them leave as fans."

Traverse City, Michigan – Before Europeans arrived, the area was a camp occupied by the Ojibwe and Ottawa people. The first permanent settlement appeared in 1839. By 1847 more people arrived to work in a successful sawmill owned by Captain Boardman. In 1895, it was incorporated as a city and has been booming ever since.

About the Author

Traverse City native **Mandy Toomey** had a career in the music industry as a country artist, touring and performing with many major label artists before settling into her new career, Motherhood. Having worked with children throughout her life, Mandy learned the importance of introducing children to books and reading at an early age. The 2001 graduate of Traverse City Central High School had no idea that becoming a mom would inspire her to write her own children's book. Mandy resides in Nashville, Tennessee with her husband, John, and daughter, Arden.

About the Illustrator

Jim DeWildt is a graduate of Kendall College of Art and Design. Jim has been a fine arts painter, commercial illustrator and graphic designer. His watercolor, oil, ink, pencil and scratchboard works (art made by scraping India ink off a clay board) can be seen in Suttons Bay where he and his wife, Manie, have a small gallery. This is Jim's fourth illustrated children's book.

www.jimdewildtgallery.com